Pl 2.5

A Note to Parents

For many children, learning math math!" is their first response — to which many parents silently add "Me, too!" Children often see adults comfortably reading and writing, but they rarely have such models for mathematics. And math fear can be catching!

The easy-to-read stories in this **Hello Reader! Math** series were written to give children a positive introduction to mathematics, and parents a pleasurable re-acquaintance with a subject that is important to everyone's life. **Hello Reader! Math** stories make mathematical ideas accessible, interesting, and fun for children. The activities and suggestions at the end of each book provide parents with a hands-on approach to help children develop mathematical interest and confidence.

Enjoy the mathematics!
• Give your child a chance to retell the story. The more familiar children are with the story, the more they will understand its mathematical concepts.
• Use the colorful illustrations to help children "hear and see" the math at work in the story.
• Treat the math activities as games to be played for fun. Follow your child's lead. Spend time on those activities that engage your child's interest and curiosity.
• Activities, especially ones using physical materials, help make abstract mathematical ideas concrete.

Learning is a messy process. Learning about math calls for children to become immersed in lively experiences that help them make sense of mathematical concepts and symbols.

Although learning about numbers is basic to math, other ideas, such as identifying shapes and patterns, measuring, collecting and interpreting data, reasoning logically, and thinking about chance, are also important. By reading these stories and having fun with the activities, you will help your child enthusiastically say "**Hello, math**," instead of "I hate math."

—Marilyn Burns
National Mathematics Educator
Author of *The I Hate Mathematics! Book*

To Andy and Nathan
— D.O.

To Jonathan, David, Benjamin, and Samuel
In my book, you guys are off the charts!
— M.L.

Copyright © 1999 by Scholastic Inc.
The activities on pages 27-32 copyright © 1999 by Marilyn Burns.
All rights reserved. Published by Scholastic Inc.
SCHOLASTIC, HELLO READER, CARTWHEEL BOOKS and associated logos
are trademarks and/or registered trademarks of Scholastic Inc.

Library of Congress Cataloging-in-Publication Data
Ochiltree, Dianne.
    Bart's amazing charts / by Diane Ochiltree; illustrated by Martin Lemelman; math activities by Marilyn Burns.
        p.   cm.— (Hello reader! Math. Level 3)
    Summary: A young boy uses different kinds of charts and graphs to present information about his life. Includes related activities.
        ISBN 0-439-09953-6
    [1. Graphic methods— Fiction.   I. Lemelman,Martin, ill.
II. Burns, Marilyn, 1941-.   III. Title.   IV. Series.

[E] — dc21

99-20216
CIP
AC

10   9   8   7   6   5   4   3   0/0   01   02   03
Printed in the U.S.A.   23
First printing, November 1999

Bart's Amazing Charts

By Dianne Ochiltree
Illustrated by Martin Lemelman
Math Activities by Marilyn Burns

Hello Reader! Math — Level 3

SCHOLASTIC INC.
New York   Toronto   London   Auckland   Sydney
Mexico City   New Delhi   Hong Kong

Joey tapped his best friend's shoulder.

"Hey, Bart! What are you doing for our class project?" he asked.

"You mean *My Life Story*?" Bart answered.

"Yeah," said Joey. "Mr. Parker said we can tell about ourselves anyway we want!"

Jessica leaned over their seat.

"I'm going to write a song.

It's called *ME-ME-ME!*" she sang.

Walter spun around.

"I'm drawing a map of my bedroom and EVERYTHING in it," he said.

Joey started talking about his plan.

Bart didn't say a word.

He had no idea what to do.

"If I don't think of something special, no one will want to hear my life story," Bart sighed.

Click, click, click, click.
Bart heard his mom working at her computer.
He went into her office. She stopped typing
and gave him a big hug.
"I've got a problem . . . I mean a project,"
Bart said. "I don't know how to start it.
Will you help me?"
"Sure," Mom answered. "Just let me finish
this sales chart first."
"What's it for?" asked Bart.

"It tells me what kinds of ice cream
sold best at the store last month," said Mom.
"Then I can figure out how much
I should order for next month."
"Are charts just for business stuff?"
asked Bart.
"You can use a chart to organize anything,"
said Mom.
"If you can count it,
measure it,
or sort it,
you can make a chart."
"Hmmm," said Bart, "that gives me
a great idea."

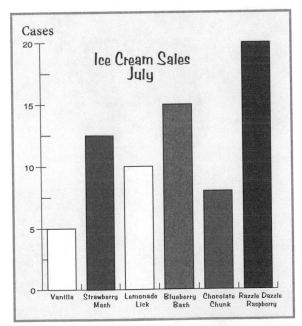

"I have to tell my life story
for a class project," Bart explained.
"And I want to do something really special.
What if I make charts that are all about ME?
They could tell about what I like and what I do
"That is a great idea," said Mom.
"Can I do them on your computer?" Bart asked
"Sure," Mom said. "You make the charts
and I'll scan them into the computer
for you. Let's try it."
Bart wrote down "Bart's Charts."
He drew a picture of himself.
Then he handed the paper to his mother.

She scanned it and it appeared on the screen.

"Amazing, huh?" said Mom.

Bart frowned.

"It needs something else," he said.

He took the paper out of the scanner
and wrote on it. Mom scanned it again.

"Much better!" said Bart.

But now what should he do?

That night Bart sat in his room
thinking about "Bart's Amazing Charts."
His little sister Katie dashed in.
"Dinnertime!" she shouted.
"Oops!" Katie bumped into Bart's bookshelf.
A big box teetered and tottered
and then tipped over.

Stacks and stacks of sports cards
flew out and covered the floor.
"Sorry," Katie whispered.
She started to pick up the cards.
"Oh, no! There must be a million cards here,"
she said.
"Actually, I think it's more like 100. . . .
Hey! you just gave me an idea
for my first chart," Bart said.
"Look, Katie, let's put them in piles like this."
Katie stacked the cards and Bart counted:
30 basketball cards,
10 football cards, and 60 baseball cards.
He grabbed the box top and a marker.
"If you can count it and sort it,
you can chart it!" Bart said.
So he did.

My Sports Card Collection

Baseball Cards- ||||| ||||| ||||| ||||| ||||| |||||
||||| ||||| ||||| ||||| ||||| |||||

Basketball Cards- ||||| ||||| ||||| ||||| ||||| |||||

Football Cards- ||||| |||||

On Friday, Dad fixed Do-It-Yourself pizzas.
"Pile on your toppings!" Dad called.
"Awesome!" said Bart. "I'm tired
of just plain cheese. What else
can I put on my pizza?"
Bart did a taste test.
He took a bite here and a nibble there.
Some toppings he liked.
And others, Yikes!
He wrote down his test results.
"If you can list it, you can chart it!" said Bart.
So he did.

Bart played basketball with Jessica
on Saturday.
"You can really slam-dunk!" he said.
"Let's see who can make the most baskets,"
said Jessica.

Bart and Jessica each got twenty turns.

If they made a basket, they got one point.

Bart kept score.

After they both took their last shots,

Bart added up the scores.

He had won!

"If you can add it, you can chart it!" said Bart.

So he did.

Bart went to Grandma Rosa's birthday party on Sunday.

All eight cousins were there.

"You're all growing up so fast," Grandma Rosa said. "Come over here and let me measure you."

Bart wondered if cousin Alex was still taller.

Grandma said, "Stand up straight!" and measured the eight cousins.

Bart took notes.

Aunt Judy helped baby Marcus stand tall.

Cousin Amy didn't need any help.

Even though Bart was younger than Alex, he was now two inches taller.

"Way to grow, Bart!" said Uncle Steve.

"If you can measure it, you can chart it!" said Bart.

So he did.

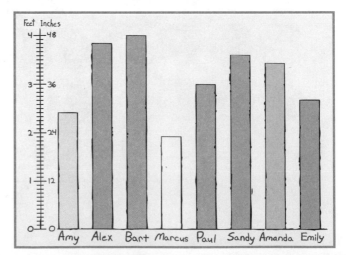

Feet Inches
5 — 60
4 — 48
3 — 36
2

At lunchtime on Monday,
Bart said, "Let's trade sandwiches!"
Jessica took out her peanut butter
and banana sandwich.
"Yuck!" said Joey.
Joey unwrapped his cheese and pickle sandwich.
"No way!" said Walter.
Walter held onto his tuna and ketchup sandwich.
Bart waved his ham and jelly sandwich.
"Too weird!" said Jessica, Joey, and Walter.
"Let's find out who's got
the strangest sandwich!" Bart said.
He flattened his lunch bag and took out a pencil.
Then he went from table to table.
All the kids in the cafeteria voted —
and NO ONE traded sandwiches with Bart.
"If you can tally it, you can chart it!" said Bart.
So he did.

Everywhere Bart went
and everything Bart did
made him think of charts!
He counted the blocks when he biked
around the neighborhood.

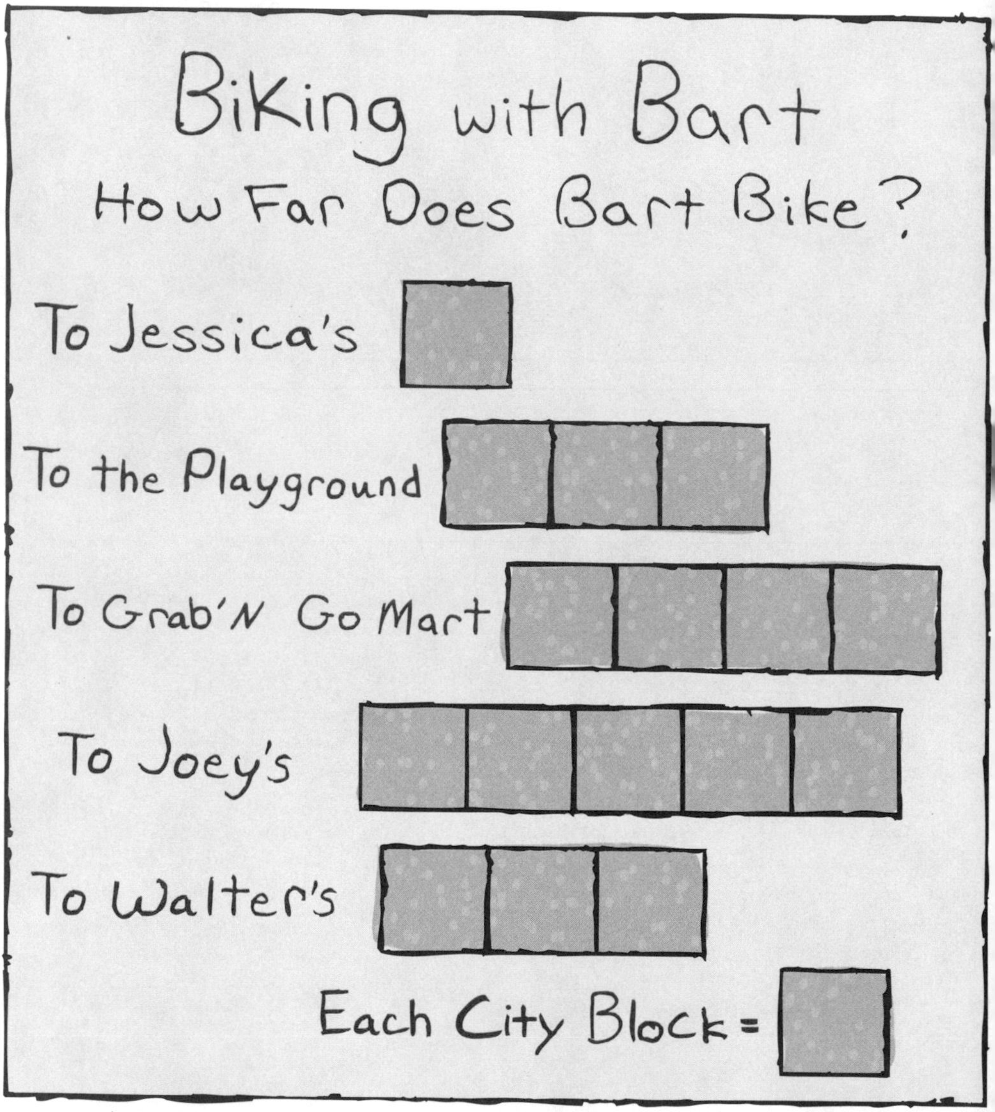

Biking with Bart
How Far Does Bart Bike?

To Jessica's

To the Playground

To Grab'N Go Mart

To Joey's

To Walter's

Each City Block =

He sorted all his different kinds of CDs.
He even kept track of his temperature
every hour when he was sick.
Every day, he gave a new chart
to his mother. She scanned it
into the computer.

A week later, all the class projects were due.
Mr. Parker called on Bart first.
He walked to the front of the classroom
empty-handed.
Everyone gave Bart a funny look.
"Did you forget something?" whispered Joey.
Bart just smiled.
"Go ahead, Bart," Mr. Parker said.
So he did.

Bart walked over to the class computer.
"Could everybody come over here?"
he asked.

"Here's my life story . . .
BART'S AMAZING CHARTS!" he cried.
Bart started clicking.

"Cool!" said Jessica.

"Wow!" said Walter.

"Amazing!" said Mr. Parker. "We should put your life story on our school web site."

Bart was really, really proud.

And no chart could measure that!

• ABOUT THE ACTIVITIES •

Graphs and charts help us present information visually and see relationships among data more easily. Examples of graphs and charts appear regularly in newspapers and magazines; creating and interpreting graphs and charts is part of your child's math learning.

Children's early experiences with graphing typically involve information about themselves and their classmates. They learn to collect data, organize it, and then represent it. They also learn to draw conclusions about information presented on graphs and charts. In this way, children are encouraged to explore basic ideas about statistics.

Bart's Amazing Charts helps introduce children to making and using charts and graphs. It helps them see the need for sorting information into categories in order to represent it graphically. Also, they see several different ways to organize information into charts and graphs. And they see the value and usefulness of using graphs to communicate.

The activities that follow give you a way to talk with your child about Bart's graphs and charts. There are also suggestions provided for graphs and charts that you can make together. Enjoy the activities and have fun with the math!

—Marilyn Burns

You'll find tips and suggestions for guiding the activities whenever you see a box like this!

Retelling the Story

Bart's Mom was looking at a graph on her computer screen. It told her about the sales of different flavors of ice cream. Look at that graph on page 7 and see if you can answer these questions.

Which ice cream flavor sold the most?

Which flavor sold the least?

How many cases of ice cream were sold altogether that month?

Which sold more: Razzle Dazzle Raspberry or Lemonade Lick? By how many cases?

What other questions can this graph help you answer?

If learning to group tally marks into fives is new for your child, he or she may still feel more comfortable counting the tally marks by ones instead of by fives. If so, after your child counts by ones, show how you get the same answer counting by fives. And then try the "Tally Ho!" activity on page 31.

✗✗✓✓

"My Sports Card Collection" is Bart's first graph. How does it help you answer these questions?

How many basketball cards does the graph show Bart has?

How many football cards does Bart have?

How many baseball cards?

How many more basketball cards would Bart need so that he had the same number of basketball and baseball cards?

✗✗✓✓

Bart then makes a chart to show the pizza toppings he likes and those he doesn't.

How many toppings did Bart put on his chart?

How many toppings does he like?

How many toppings does Bart think are awful?

For each section of "Retelling the Story," ask your child to use the information on the appropriate graph or chart to answer the questions. If he or she is confused by any of the questions, ask what your child can tell from the graph. This will give you information about what makes sense to your child at this stage. Then return to that question at a later time.

✗✗✓✓

Bart and Jessica keep track of their basketball shots. They each took twenty turns and scored one point for each basket they made.

How many points did Jessica score?

How many points did Bart score?

How many more points did Bart score than Jessica?

How many baskets did they each miss?

How many baskets did they make altogether?

✗✗✓✓

Grandma Rosa measured the heights of Bart and all his cousins. Bart took notes and then made a bar graph. Use the graph to answer these questions.

Who is the tallest cousin?

Who is the shortest?

How tall is Bart? Marcus? Amy?

How much taller than Emily is Bart?

How does Bart's height compare with Alex's height?

What else does this graph tell you?

✗✗✓✓

Bart takes a survey at lunchtime. Can you use it to find the answers to these questions?

How many kids did Bart survey?

What does the graph show students thought about the four weird sandwiches?

Which sandwich do you think is the strangest?

✗✗✓✓

Bart figures out how many blocks he bikes when he goes to visit Jessica, to the playground, to the Grab 'N Go Mart, to Joey's house, and to Walter's house.

Which of Bart's friends lives closest to him?

Which is closer to Bart's house — the playground or the Grab 'N Go Mart?

How many blocks farther is it to Joey's house than to Jessica's house?

Tally Ho!

Bart used tally marks to show how many of each kind of sports card he has. His tally marks are in groups of five — four tally marks going up and down and the fifth tally mark going across.

My Sports Card Collection

Baseball Cards — 卌 卌 卌 卌 卌 卌 卌 卌 卌 卌 卌 卌

Basketball Cards — 卌 卌 卌 卌 卌 卌 卌

Football Cards — 卌 卌

Can you count by fives — 5, 10, 15, 20, 25, 30, and so on? Can you count to 100 by fives? Can you count higher?

It's easy to count by fives if you remember this pattern: all of the numbers end with a five or a zero. And because it's easy to count by fives, it makes sense to organize tally marks into fives.

Use tally marks to make a chart that shows how old everyone in your family is. Write each person's name down and then put tally marks next to the name to show that person's age. Finally, put a title on your chart.

Your Own Pizza Survey

Make your own chart of pizza toppings that you like and those you don't. Then see how your chart is like Bart's and how it is different.

Statistics Search

Look through some magazines or newspapers and see if you can find any charts or graphs. What statistics do they give you?

All About Me

Try making some charts and graphs that tell things about you and your family or friends. What sorts of things can you count, list, measure, sort, or tally?